This book belongs to:

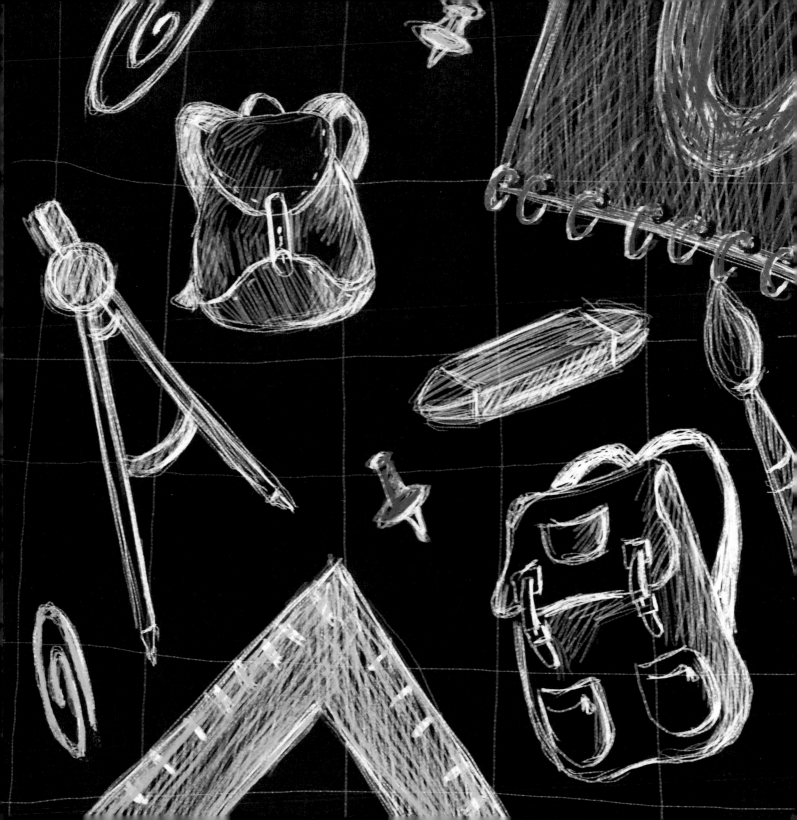

Ellie the Elephant Makes New Friends at School

Printed in the United States of America
First Printing: August, 2018
www.apriltalebooks.com

SCHOOL

by Agnes Green
illustrated by Viktoriia Mykhalevych

Hi! My name is Ellie. And this is my first day at school

I woke up this morning,
as happy as could be,
Excited for the day ahead, dressing hurriedly,
I raced downstairs and kissed my mom, on my
first day of school.

Although I knew I'd miss her, I thought school
would be cool!
The thought of making brand new friends and
learning loads of things
Filled my heart with happiness and
I began to sing.

I sang along the sidewalk and,
across the railroad track
My brand new shoes were laced up tight,
my pack upon my back,
But as the building came in view,
the closer that I got

I started to think maybe,
I'd really rather not
Go into that strange classroom
what if I don't belong?
My tummy felt all icky,
what happened to my song?

Yet, go I must, so on I went,
pretending to be brave
I walked into the classroom,
I smiled and I waved
The teacher showed me to my desk,
"before we can begin,

tell us all about yourself",
she asked me with a grin.
My name is Ellie Elephant and
I love chocolate cake!
And riding on a tricycle and
learning how to bake

But when I sat upon my chair,
it quickly broke in half!
That started Perry Puppy,
and all the rest to laugh.

The teacher said they shouldn't laugh,
that kindness was the rule.

That each and every animal is
a friend here at our school
Although they stopped their laughing,
things went from bad to worse
As I walked past everybody,
I tripped and spilled my purse

Later on, at play time,
I tried to get the blocks,
I really didn't mean to,
break open the toy box.

Again the other children,
began to laugh at me.
I hung my head in shame,

and sat beneath a tree.
My teacher saw me sitting
so sadly by myself
She offered me a special book,
off of her book shelf.

Still I was so sad and lonely,
it wasn't any fun
To be so big and awkward,
cast out by everyone.
But as I sat there thinking,
what would become of me,
The other children's basketball
got stuck up in the tree.
I stood up to retrieve it,
not even thinking twice,
Cause, though I am an Elephant,
I'm very kind and nice.

The other kids were happy,
they clapped their hands with glee.
Then Pablo Pig asked,
"Ellie, won't you come play with me?"
I tossed the ball to Pablo,
and joined in with them all.

It really didn't matter, short,
wide, tall, big or small.
The others danced round me,
and I joined in the fun,
Before the day was over,
I was friends with everyone!

So when the school day ended,
I skipped home all the way
Then told my mom about my friends
and of the games we play
She asked about my teacher,
what was my favorite thing

I love the books and stories
and the songs we got to sing.
But the thing that made me happiest
and makes me really grin
Is knowing that tomorrow
I'll get to go again!!

58493582R00015

Made in the USA
Middletown, DE
06 August 2019